GRUMPY SPECIAL OPS BEAR: EPISODE 1

BEAR ELITE SHIFTERS

SEDONA VENEZ

WANT FREE SEDONA VENEZ BOOKS?

Sign up for Sedona Venez's Newsletter and receive FREE BOOKS. In addition to the free stories, you will also get special pricing, exclusive previews and news of new releases.

GET A FREE SEDONA VENEZ BOOK!

Join Sedona's mailing list to be the first to know of new releases, free books, special prices and other author giveaways.

https://sedonavenez.com/free-book

CHAPTER 1

TRINITY

THE DOOR SLIPPED OPEN, and air rushed into the compartment. We were high in the sky, the land below specks of farms and roads. This always left me breathless, but not in a bad way.

I was definitely doing this by choice.

The adrenaline pumped through my veins as I pictured myself jumping out of the plane. My palms started to sweat. The wind blew across my face as I pulled my goggles down and grinned from ear to ear.

Moving forward, I shouted through the door in my excitement, "Damn, I love this shit!"

I checked over my parachute pull one last

time. With a salute to the men running the show standing near the doors to assist the rest of the jumpers and me, I leaped out of the airplane and tumbled through the air.

"Yeah!" I yelled in triumph as I went.

Skydiving had always been one of my favorite activities to do with clients who wanted a real nail-biting rush. Shit, I knew it always started my blood pumping. I was an unabashed thrill junkie.

Gazing up, I saw the rest of my party taking off after me into the open sky, one after the other.

Soon the air filled with falling rainbow-colored bodies in jumpsuits. They hollered and screamed as they plunged, and I once again realized how damn lucky I was. This was my highly prized corner office, with a sky-blue backdrop all around me. The wind caressed my skin, and I had all the freedom that came from falling through the air, knowing that only my parachute would stop me from crashing into the ground.

Everything about my life was perfect—well, almost perfect.

I enjoyed the fall.

When we were at the point where we

should pull our chutes, I signaled the rest of the party. Once they all got the message, I pulled my rip cord. My chute opened beautifully, and I glanced over my shoulder to watch all the others open. We coasted on the wind, guiding ourselves toward the designated landing area.

A few minutes later, I touched down smoothly, running a bit to let my parachute fall behind me. I waited for the rest of the party to do the same.

The second we were all on the ground, one jumper pulled off his goggles and waved at me. His tanned face glowed from the jump, and he was grinning like a boy on Christmas morning. "Trinity, that was by far the best thing I've ever done. I can't believe I've never thought to do this."

I laughed, removing my goggles and hood. "I'm so happy you loved it, Neal. Now you need to do this every few months, and you and your board will never be as stressed out over profit margins and new product launches again."

Neal—the tall, lean CEO who'd hired me to lead his group on this little adventure—laughed so hard he doubled over. "I might take you up on that—as long as you're there to jump with us." His eyes skated over my body with interest. "Now, if I could get you to agree to have dinner and drinks with me tonight..." He grinned.

Truth be told, I actually got a kick out of being around him, which was new for me. The majority of my billionaire clients were cocky and obnoxious, spending most of our outings trying to grope me or boring me with how big their bank accounts were. Neal was quite the opposite. He was a big lovable guy who enjoyed flirting with me, but there was no way I would break my no-fraternizing-with-clients rule.

His fingers caressed my elbow. "I can regale you with tales of my many adventures in slaying snarling board members consumed with world domination. And you can explain again why such a bright and beautiful woman like you isn't in a relationship."

I pressed my lips together as I looked pointedly at his roving fingers. He snatched back his hand.

"As much as I love your company, Neal, I'll have to decline the dinner and drinks invitation," I answered, stepping away from him slightly. "Until our next adventure."

We shook hands as the rest of the group came over to say their goodbyes to me as well. When I finished thanking them, three black SUVs drove up to take them all back to the city.

I steered toward the huge SUV where my assistant, Halle, was waiting, smiling as usual.

Halle jumped out of the driver's side before bouncing over to me. "Damn, that was a pretty wicked dive. I watched most of it from the live feed on your helmet."

"You have to try it," I answered. "How about this weekend?" I waggled my brows.

Halle shook her head. "Hard pass. You know I don't have the stomach. I'll stick to being your well-paid minion."

I loved working with Halle, a fresh-out-of-college student who'd always go wide-eyed with every stunt I finished. It made me miss the young exuberance I'd had coming into this business years ago, but at thirty-six, I'd done a lot of living, both good and bad.

"All right. But you don't know what you're missing," I joked while stretching my muscles, which had built over the years from performing stunts. I stepped out of my flight suit. All I wanted was a long, hot soak, a glass of wine, and a marathon of mind-numbing reality shows.

I looked over at Halle. "Is that it for the day?"

Halle laughed as she reached into the back seat for a small duffel. "You wish. We're going to dinner to meet with your new clients. They walked in this morning and were able to get a meeting right away. They must have some deep pockets if they could do that."

It usually took clients a few weeks, even months, before they could meet with Hector —my peer and other guide—or me. A lot of planning was involved in these trips. Not to mention, we would run background checks on the clients to ensure people like me wouldn't be going on trips with killers or members of a mob. It took preparation and lots of money to get something like this going.

Whatever the clients were paying, it must've been a hell of a lot. I hoped we at least completed the background checks. I'd prefer not to be stuck with a bunch of psychos on a dangerous adventure where anything could go wrong.

Halle jumped behind the wheel.

"How many in the group?" I asked while kicking off my sneakers.

"Seven."

I frowned. "I've never taken so many clients as a solo guide. Can't we reschedule this until Hector gets back from his honeymoon?" Normally, by myself, I'd take only four people to ensure the safety of the group and to ensure that I had time to dedicate to each client.

"The bosses say that you can decline this job, but they're offering to pay you double for this trip with a hefty bonus."

My eyes widened. "Holy shit! Hell yes, I'm taking this job." It would mean more money in my nest egg for retirement. But I also knew that I'd have to work harder to ensure everyone in the group's safety, which I was more than capable of doing. "These clients must be VIPs. Do you have any idea who they are?"

"They work for some finance company— at least I think they do. I didn't get to hear much before I was told to come get you." Halle's fingers played nervously on the steering wheel. "I saw them when they came in though, and... Trinity, they're unusual."

"Lovely. They'd better not be assholes," I groused while tugging my dress pants over my tight yoga bottoms. I slipped my suit jacket over the snug black Lycra tank top. My look was complete when I pulled my dark brown cinnamon hair from my bun and shook it out, allowing it to cascade around my shoulders. Tossing all my discarded items into the bag, I climbed into the SUV.

Halle shook her head. "I wasn't thinking asshole weird, more like creepy. There were seven of them, but only one of them ever said a word. It was like the others were scared to speak."

I unhappily pursed my lips. "That's bizarre. Are they new employees?"

Halle shrugged. "No idea. The whole situation was strange. Though the guy who did talk was pretty fucking hot." She waggled her eyebrows at me. "Rough around the edges, but that beard stubble... Man, I wish I were going with you."

"Interesting," I retorted. "Stilettos in the back?"

"Of course." Halle glanced at me sideways. "It was the first thing I checked."

"I trained you well, grasshopper."

Reaching into the back seat, I took hold of my sleek stilettos and slipped my feet into them. "I only hope you're wrong about these clients. I really don't feel like dealing with a bunch of fucking idiots on a dangerous trip. One horrific experience was enough to last me a damn lifetime."

CHAPTER 2

TRINITY

I RUSHED THROUGH THE DOOR, darting my eyes around. Looking over at Halle, I inquired, "Do you see them?"

Halle pointed to the guy pacing back and forth. "There's one of them. I believe his name is Josh Price."

My eyes locked on him as we sauntered toward him.

Goddamn. He is pretty hot.

He smiled, glancing at Halle and then me. "I was wondering if I got the time wrong."

"That would be my fault," I explained, stepping forward with my hand out to shake his. "Trinity Holiday, the guide the agency has sent to you and your group, Mr. Price. I apologize for being late. I jumped out of an airplane not too long ago."

He grinned, holding my hand longer than necessary. "Sounds like you've had quite the day."

An unexpected jolt shot through my fingers, and I quickly pulled them away.

His smile slipped before his lips tilted up again. "I'm looking forward to our trip together, and so is the rest of my group. We're just right over here," he replied, leading the way to his table.

Halle and I followed him through a maze of tables in the busy restaurant, dodging servers with trays and businesspeople who'd had too much to drink.

"So," Halle whispered before we arrived at the table. "What do you think? Hot but creepy, right?"

I scrunched up my nose. "Hot, but not my type, and something's definitely different about him. But I'm not sure I'd call him creepy." *More like unnerving.*

The last time I'd felt like this, lions in the great African plains had surrounded me. I'd been out in the wild with clients when we'd come across a lion pride. In that moment of staring death in the face, I had felt just like this... as if I was in danger of being mauled to death at any moment.

I shook my head and tried to concentrate on the meeting at hand. "We'll talk about this later," I whispered to Halle.

When we eventually stopped, I took a long look at all of them and wondered why the hair along the back of my neck was suddenly standing on end. The impression from earlier intensified tenfold, and I tried not to wince. Glancing around, I looked for an air vent but didn't see one.

After the introductions to four men and two women, Halle and I sat down at the table and started in on the details of the trip.

"So," I began with a forced smile. "I hear from Halle that you're looking to go on an adventure in Alaska?" I arched a brow. "A four-week camping trip, starting the first week of December? Quite an outing to take for beginners like yourselves."

They all nodded, but Josh spoke. "Yes, we thought a get-together would help us bond. Some of us are new to the company. What better way to get to know your new colleagues than a camping trip out in the Alaskan wild?

This has been a big year for us, and I thought it was time to celebrate our achievements uniquely."

I scowled at his lighthearted speech. They all seemed excited, but none of them looked like they were used to surviving in the outdoors. The deep woods of Alaska is a rugged place, with no room for overzealous white-collar executives. Things could always take a quick turn for the worse, especially coming into this season. Huge snowfalls weren't uncommon this time of year, and that brought a chance for storms and dangerously low temperatures.

"This isn't just some ordinary camping trip you want me to plan, and I need to make sure you all understand this," I emphasized, laying my hands flat on the table. "The wilderness in Alaska is dangerous. If you're not careful, if you don't play by the rules and follow my lead, you could end up hurt or dead." I stared them down.

Except for Halle, everyone at the table seemed to twitch at my words, but none of them appeared worried.

Who are these fucking people?

From what Halle had explained, they had

no experience with a trip like this, yet none showed the slightest bit of apprehension. I waited to see if anyone would respond to my words.

Once again, only Josh answered me. "We understand. Now, let's go over our itinerary, shall we? We have a lot to plan and little time to get it all ready to go."

I nodded, a bit unsettled by their reactions, as I tried to silence the warning bells jingling in my head. Every fiber of my body screamed that this trip was a clusterfuck waiting to happen.

Beckoning the server over, I said, "Please bring your wine menu." I was going to need all the liquid courage I could get to soothe my suddenly frayed nerves. I just hoped my gut instincts were wrong.

CHAPTER 3
TRINITY

THE SKY WAS dark as pellets of icy snow beat against my body. My teeth chattered loudly from my drenched clothes as I pushed through the dense forest.

Despair and confusion clouded my mind. Where am I?

With my body dragging, I felt like I had been walking forever with no destination. My feet slogged through the snow mixed with mud. The farther I plowed into the wilderness, the more concerned I became.

Keep going, Trinity, *I repeated over and over in my head.*

Pushing one snow-laden branch out of the path, I trod into a big clearing. I took one step and heard the ice cracking beneath my foot, then plunged into the frigid water.

"Help," I croaked into the darkness.

I clawed at the edge of the hole but to no avail. It crumbled under my fingers as I sloshed about. I was becoming hypothermic as tears slid down my cheeks.

I was going to die—alone.

"Please," I whimpered.

The trees around the clearing rustled, and a gigantic bear bounded through it. It roared while racing toward me. On its back were streaks of golden fur. Its teeth were terrifyingly huge, but its eyes... They were sky blue.

I shook my head in confusion. This couldn't be right. Bears didn't have blue eyes.

The bear sidled up to me, tilting its head in inquiry. I almost swallowed my tongue when it reared up on its hind legs and growled. I shouted out in terror.

I sat straight up in bed, gasping, as I'd done for the past several nights. The dreams had become more intense, and each time the same bear would appear.

I swung my legs over the edge of the mattress and leaned forward with my elbows on my knees and my face in my hands. My heart was racing as I tried to shake off the overwhelming uneasiness, thinking these dreams were a negative omen of things to come.

Something was terribly wrong, and I didn't know what it was. I had a bad feeling it was linked to my upcoming trip with Josh Price and his team.

My final meeting with them had been one of the oddest interactions I'd ever experienced with any client. After we had gone through the itinerary, he'd wanted to get to know me a bit. He'd asked about my family and my friends and if my absence from home during the holiday season would be an issue. Most clients wouldn't ask about my personal life, and I really didn't like it when people pried. I'd managed not to tell him anything about myself because, frankly, my life wasn't that interesting.

My story was like most other orphans. I hadn't seen the point of explaining where I'd come from. Honestly, I didn't care that as a baby I'd been abandoned and brought up in a series of foster homes. My childhood strengthened me. And being a bit of a loner didn't define me.

I hoped I'd last the whole four weeks and not come back with bruised and broken clients for my bosses to deal with. They'd gone twenty years without a lawsuit. I was pretty sure they'd fire my ass if I were the one to break that streak.

The best-case scenario would be if Josh and his team tapped out before the four weeks were over. They wouldn't be the first clients to do so, and that was why my bosses had a no-refund policy.

Hence, I had a contingency plan. If Josh and his team couldn't make it through the whole four weeks, they would have to handle their own transportation out of the wild.

CHAPTER 4

TRINITY

DAY ONE OF THE TRIP, I tried to relax as the helicopter dropped us off at our starting point. In four weeks, we would circle back to this point to be picked up. I'd planned everything, so as long as we stuck to our schedule, we'd be on time.

Halle handed my pack to me and glanced around at the rest of the group. "I wish I could stay with you. Some of these guys are hot. Damn, even the two women are pretty attractive," she whispered. "And they're all freaking rich. That's always a big plus. I took a glance at the check Mr. Price wrote. Holy shit, Trinity. If you were looking for a sexy billionaire, I'd say he's your man."

"I'm not interested," I proclaimed, trying to keep it light. But the hair on the back of my neck was up again. I was used to that sensation when I was getting ready to leap out of an airplane or go bungee jumping but never when I was just standing around people.

I'd noticed my apprehension elevated mostly around Josh.

Over the past couple of meetings, I'd gotten the same weird reaction when I was near him, but all the background checks had come back clean. He was the new CEO of a Manhattan-based company that was doing extremely well. And as my bosses had reminded me, he was bound to do business with them again if he was satisfied with this trip. They'd drilled it into my head that I should ensure Mr. Price had a wonderful time so he'd come back and tell the rest of his board members and friends about it. They'd do anything to draw in more rich clients. If I weren't being paid as much as I was for this trip, I would've swallowed my fake smile and told my bosses to fuck off.

"Yeah, well," Halle responded with a shrug, "have fun without me. Everything is in your bag. You have the satellite phone, and the walkie-talkies are already set to the local channels of the Alaska state park rangers. I think I also packed enough first aid kits to save you from a bear attack."

I glowered. "Really? If one of us is attacked by a bear, I don't think bandages will help."

She snickered quietly. "You never know. All right, it looks like your group is ready to go." She gave me a quick hug and then waved goodbye to everyone else. "I'll see you all in four weeks."

We watched Halle get back into the helicopter, and then it took off.

I turned around to address the group and flinched when I saw Josh watching me intently, almost hungrily. For a second, I thought about calling Halle back, but then he smiled and came to stand beside me. It was a weird shift, and I tried not to let it bother me. I wasn't exactly a greedy person, but my bosses had been paying me well for five years. I could handle a few peculiar people for four weeks.

"Trinity, we'll follow your lead," Josh announced.

I nodded and cleared my throat, hoping

the sudden nervousness would disappear once we were under way. "Everyone has their packs on tight? We've got a few miles to go today before we get to our first campsite."

"I think we'll be all right," Josh stated.

"We'll keep up. If not, just leave the newbie for the bears," Boyle, one of the other associates, drawled with a wink as he gave a friendly shove to who I thought was Owen.

Boyle was large, taller and burlier than Josh. A scar ran up the side of his right cheek and disappeared into his ebony hairline. I'd noticed it yesterday, but today it stood out from his harshly lined face.

"Owen's got enough meat on his bones to slow down a bear."

I sighed and reminded myself to maintain my cool. They were new to this. I would have to give them a few days to understand what they had gotten themselves into.

I eyed the entire team—Josh, Boyle, Ian, Owen, Brian, Maggie, and Brenda. "If a bear attacks us, we won't be leaving anyone behind," I scolded. "You'll do exactly as I say and nothing more if you want to live."

"Oh, come on, Trinity. We're just having a little fun," Josh told me.

"There will be plenty of fun, but I need to know all of you will also take your safety seriously. This is not a joke. We're not in some movie. This is reality, and if one of us gets seriously injured, it could require hours or days for help to reach us, if they can reach us at all," I stated.

Josh turned to his companions and raised his eyebrows. "Agreed. Right, everyone? Trinity's in charge. We do exactly as she says."

For a second, I thought I saw every one of them bow their heads to Josh before he turned back to me and nodded. I read that as the signal they were ready to set out. I pulled out my compass to ensure we would head northeast toward our objective.

Josh and his team talked as we hiked through the wild. I listened but concentrated on just getting to the campsite. Their conversation really wasn't making much sense to me anyway. They continued speaking about business back home and getting things completed in time before the big day. I didn't want to eavesdrop. I needed to keep my ears tuned in to other noises around us.

Just get through day one, I repeated over and over as I trekked up a steep hill.

I wanted nothing to happen, but I also wanted to make sure they all knew what they were getting into for the next four weeks. Besides, it wasn't as if they would really rough it. The only thing they had to do when we reached the campsite was set up the tents. A stash of supplies was at each spot where we would camp over the next four weeks thanks to the money Josh had supplied to the company I worked for.

It had taken almost two months just to get everything set up. Josh had been specific about every part of this trip. Not that I minded. Each phase had been planned out well.

A few hours into the hike, I got a bit tired and was ready to call for a brief break, but none of them were. Not one of them was out of breath, looked exhausted, or even red in the face. I was in good shape, but my thighs, particularly my quads, burned from the exertion.

"Anyone need a break?" I called out anyway. "Ready to grab some water and a quick snack before we head onward?"

"Sure," Josh agreed. "Break, everyone."

They all removed their packs and found seats on the ground as I removed mine and pulled out a granola bar. I walked a few yards away and checked our surroundings. So far, everything was fine. The temperature was chilly but not overly frigid. I had checked the weather reports for this week, and no storms had been on the radar. The Alaska state park rangers had promised they'd get ahold of me somehow if something big headed our way.

Thank goodness the trip was going well so far, but that wasn't what worried me. I wasn't sure why, but I wasn't as comfortable as I normally would be out in the wilderness, away from the city.

"So how are we doing so far?" Josh asked.

I turned, finishing a gulp of water, and forced a grin onto my face. "Well, no one's passed out yet or fallen into a hole, so I'd say everyone's doing pretty well for amateurs." I played with my water bottle for a second before glancing up at him. "Are you sure none of you guys have hiking experience?"

"Not that they've told me about. They're just really excited to be out here."

I nodded, but I wasn't convinced. "I think it's time to get moving again. You want to tell everyone to pack up? We won't break again until we arrive at the first encampment.

Maybe we'll do some fishing for dinner tonight."

"Sounds good. I'll tell the others." Josh headed to his group and told them to pack up and move out.

A few minutes later, they were back on the trail, following me through the wild.

CHAPTER 5

FERGUS

MY BREATH CREATED tiny white puffs in the cold air. I crouched down under the tree cover and stared at the multiple sets of footprints. A large party with five or maybe six individuals had passed through the spot not too long ago.

I took a deep breath and smelled the dense forest air. Something wasn't right about the stench. But until I had a visual, I had nothing to go on except these tracks, and they told me little about who was in this traveling party.

"Beta to Alpha, have you found a visual?" Cutter's voice came over my radio.

I pressed my earpiece tighter against my ear as I clicked the button on the radio at my shoulder. "Alpha to Beta, that's a negative. Footprints heading north. Multiples, but no visual. I repeat, no visual."

"Orders?"

"Meet me at the first rendezvous point. Alpha out." I clicked off the radio and straightened.

I gripped the rifle tightly in my hands before slinging it over my shoulder. With two shoulder holsters, which carried at least three knives, I was prepared for anything that might cross my path. However, a wild animal wasn't what I wanted to find today.

People had made these tracks.

I scanned the trees, but I saw no other tracks besides the footprints. Growling deep in annoyance, I trudged toward the rendezvous point to meet up with the rest of my team. Perhaps they had more information to help me understand why this mission was quickly turning from simple to dangerous. But we had our orders, and I never missed my mark—ever.

A few minutes of heavy hiking and I was

at the river. From what I could tell, the group had passed this way, out of the neutral territory. The rest of my team, Cutter and Grant, stood alert, waiting for me.

My second-in-command, Cutter, stepped forward and nodded toward the north. He casually flung a knife up and down as he said, "From what we can tell, they're setting up camp about three miles that way."

"You had a visual?" I demanded.

"No, but a campsite is there and ready to go. We waited for most of the day, but there's been no sign of them so far," Cutter explained. "What do you think, Fergus?"

I rubbed my jaw and gazed across the river. "We'll stake out the camp but keep our distance. I want to be certain of how many people we're dealing with."

"Understood," Cutter agreed.

"Let's get moving, Grant," I ordered.

Grant, the third and final member of my team, didn't answer. He gazed toward the tree line with a dark look, his tanned fingers raking across his stark-white hair. His solemn silence was normal. But out of the three of us, he was by far more dangerous to cross, which was why I'd recruited him for my team. Grant was loyal to a fault, and he never backed down.

I trekked onward, leading Cutter and Grant toward a ridge overlooking the campsite. By nightfall, I hoped we'd have a visual of our target.

CHAPTER 6

TRINITY

BY THE TIME the group and I reached the campsite, the sun was going down, but there was still enough light to fish. So once we dumped our gear and got a fire going, I led them down to the riverbank. When I turned to instruct them on the proper way to fish, I saw they were already casting lines and teasing one another about who would catch the bigger fish for dinner.

I glowered, but I kept my mouth closed.

I decided when we reached the next site, I was going to call Halle to find out if she could dig up any other information on them. They obviously had more experience than they had acknowledged.

I'd just eased myself down onto a slab of rock I'd picked as my fishing spot when I got a weird feeling in the nether part of my belly. Peeking about, I winced when I found Josh staring at me so intensely the hair on the nape of my neck stood on end, as usual with them. For a second, I felt the pressing need to move away, but then it died as he worked his way over to me.

"Mind if I join you?" he asked.

"Help yourself," I replied as he plopped down next to me. "If we catch nothing, there's food locked in a metal crate in one tent."

"I'm certain they'll hook something at some point. So tell me more about yourself. Besides the fact that you like to jump out of airplanes and take random people on trips into the wilderness," he added with a wink.

I rammed my fishing pole into the dirt beside the rock. "There's not much else to say."

"Oh, there has to be something. Does your love of adventure come from your parents?"

An old anger raised its head, but I promptly stomped it down. *Relax, Trinity. He's just curious, not prying.*

There was no reason for me to bite his

head off, but if he kept pushing, I was going to go straight New York crazy on his ass.

"I was abandoned as a kid, and I grew up in foster homes."

"Sad to hear that."

I shrugged and smiled. "It's all right. I turned out fine."

"So you don't know who your parents are?"

"Nope, never tried to find them either," I answered. "Figured if they didn't want me, then I didn't want them."

"I can understand that. So where does your adventurous spirit come from?"

I turned to him. "Don't you think that's a little personal?"

Immediately, he held up his hands. "Sorry. I didn't realize it was a touchy subject."

"It's not a sensitive topic." Taking a deep breath, I let it out, straining to get a grip on my mood. "I apologize. I'm just not good with conversation. Usually I don't talk with the people I go on trips with."

He just laughed. "Too busy falling out of airplanes?"

"Something like that," I replied. "What

about you? I know that your company's head-quarters are in Manhattan. Are you a native New Yorker?"

"No. I move around a lot."

"Hmm... Lots of traveling?"

"No. Lots of running away from the law."

I stiffened instantly.

He just snickered. "It's not what you think. I left home when I was young. Bounced around for a bit and got into heaps of trouble." He nodded over in Boyle's direction. "I met Boyle along the way. We were both head-strong and loners, so it wasn't an easy friend-ship, but we had a great deal in common. Years later, here we are, two misfit million-aires sitting in the middle of nowhere, camping."

I sat in silence, sorting through Josh's story. A lot of it rang true, but the slivers of information he'd left out were troubling. I watched two others catch a fish each, big ones, and I shook my head.

They've never been fishing before, my ass.

I exhaled sharply. Maybe I was reading too much into Josh's and his team's behavior. Frankly, it wasn't any of my business. As long as they had a good time and no one got hurt or killed, I'd get paid a hefty bonus at the end of the trip.

After we caught a few more fish, we headed back to the campsite and made dinner. Sitting in the firelight, I couldn't help the laughter that slipped out at their antics and joking. They seemed more like family than coworkers, only they looked nothing alike. I glanced across the campground and grimaced when my eyes swiftly locked with Josh's intense stare.

Shit.

He was getting creepy again. If he kept watching me like a hawk, I was going to say something, and it wouldn't be nice.

The sun had gone down, and darkness surrounded us as the bugs came out to play. I shooed away a flying insect and caught Josh's eyes once more. He nodded to me, and I tried to smile back, but my lips wouldn't move.

His freaky eyes had an abnormal amber glow. I peered around the campsite and nearly choked. All their eyes were glowing. Their sheer beauty fascinated me. Suddenly my mind became cloudy, my vision fuzzy, and then my brain went blank.

I blinked at him in confusion.

Where the hell am I?

My hands trembled as my thoughts became so jumbled that the harder I tried to unravel them, the more difficult it became to clear my head.

Taking a deep, cleansing breath, I concentrated on settling my mind, and the confusion ebbed away.

What the fuck was that?

Never in my life had I experienced something so disorientating and scary. I stood up on wobbly legs. "Guys, it's been a long day. I'm turning in early. Allow the fire to burn down to embers."

I didn't even wait for a response before turning on my heel and hightailing it away.

CHAPTER 7

FERGUS

WHAT THE FUCK?

I whiffed the air once more to be certain.

A human female?

I stared down at the camp.

We were high on a ridge overlooking the group. Cutter and Grant were spread out farther away. We needed an exact number, and for damn sure, we didn't need a human in the middle of this shit.

I shook my head in disbelief.

Did she even know what she was doing? No—did she recognize who the hell these people actually were?

"Beta to Alpha," Cutter drawled.

"Alpha. Go," I snarled, growing angrier by

the damn second.

"Do my eyes deceive me, or is that an unknown with our group?"

"It is." I stayed where I was, lying flat on the ground, watching the woman get up and disappear into her tent.

Then I eyed the primary target, calmly sitting there on a log, watching the woman's tent hungrily. This human female was of no concern to me. Protecting humans from harm was the responsibility of the Protectors—hybrids whose job it was to hunt and kill feral and outlaw shifters that either killed a human or were a threat to human society. I was only focused on my target.

Damn. Should we move in while she's out of the way?

No.

The noise would draw her out, and I wasn't about to have innocent blood on my hands. If she got in the way when we made our move, there was no guarantee she wouldn't get taken out with the rest of them.

I growled. "We can't move in until we know who she is. Tell Grant to take some pics, and then we'll set up camp for the night."

"Got it."

CHAPTER 8

TRINITY

A FEW MORE DAYS HAD GONE BY, and Josh had opened up a bit more about his life. He and I had a lot more in common than I'd originally thought. We were both cast-aways who had grown up with no family.

I had to admit I wasn't used to being around people who actually talked to me. Josh and his team had been attempting to get to know who I was instead of just treating me as their guide.

As we continued on our trek through the wilderness, Josh had been walking with me each day. In fact, he'd been bonding more with me than with the rest of the group. And he seemed less like another rich asshole who was trying to hit on me.

We stopped by a stream for a break as week one was slowly coming to a close.

Perplexingly, I found myself drawn to Josh.

His muscles tensed as he crouched down to refill his water bottle, and I felt my chest tighten. Something about him was both intriguing and frightening.

"I can feel you staring at me from over here," he joked without turning my way.

I cleared my throat, mentally kicking myself. "Sorry. I was just thinking about something."

"Oh yeah? And what's that?" He stood and headed toward me. He took a swig of water, and it ran down his stubbled chin.

I watched him until I realized I was doing it again, and I shook my head. "Nothing. Just wondering if your group would like to try their hand at hunting some small game for dinner?"

"I'm sure they wouldn't mind a few pointers from you." He wiped the water from his chin with his sleeve and winked.

"I doubt they'll need any such help from me."

He shrugged his muscular shoulders. "Never know. We've never met anyone like you before." He reached his hand up and tucked the hair that had fallen from my bun back behind my ear. "Your skin is even more beautiful in this light."

"Thanks," I croaked.

What the hell is wrong with me?

I took a step back. "Let's get moving!" I yelled to the team. "We'll hunt for game as we head to the next site. We'll be at that one for a few nights," I announced. Then I turned and continued forward, knowing they'd catch up quickly enough.

CHAPTER 9

TRINITY

WE'D JUST FINISHED a dinner that included rabbits and even a few geese. Their hunting skills hadn't surprised me. I was just confused as to why they had all tried to act so naive when they seemed to know more than I did about surviving in the outdoors.

Boyle and Owen were the ones who had brought in the rabbits. When I'd asked how they'd caught them, Boyle just winked, and Owen smirked. The two women in the group, Maggie and Brenda, had returned with the geese. But as far as I knew, none of them had a weapon besides knives.

So how the hell did they kill them?

Josh, Ian, and Brian had gone with me. I'd

shown them how to make traps to catch rabbits and then how to kill them quickly and efficiently once we had caught them. I'd thought I'd heard them snicker behind me, but when I'd turned around, they had been solemn and watching me intently.

As the evening got darker, I wandered away from camp, observing the stars from beneath the trees. They were so beautiful, clear, and crisp. There was no light pollution to dim them. If I could live out here forever, I would. But every now and again, I wanted to hear some city noise.

I'd been alone all my life, and I wasn't about to spend the rest of my existence wandering through the wilderness with no one around at all. I could do it for a while, maybe, but not forever.

Away from the fire, I was cold, so I wrapped my arms around my body. I didn't want to go back to the campsite yet. I needed a few moments to get a grip on my thoughts before they spiraled too far out of control.

Josh and his team weren't threatening. They were just unusual. I'd dealt with plenty of oddball people before. Hell, I was one too.

Few people would consider what I did daily as normal.

A smile lit my lips as I thought about the past few years of working for the agency and all the places I'd gone, exotic locations very few people had ever heard of.

The life I led was incredible.

I noticed a few clouds rolling in from the west, and I took a deep breath and then exhaled, letting go of all the stress that had built up since this trip started.

Everything is going to be fine. It always is.

There had been only one time when things hadn't gone according to plan, and I would think about it every time before I set out on a trip.

"You seem to be deep in thought," Josh remarked right behind me.

I jumped, startled. "Shit."

"Sorry, I didn't mean to sneak up on you."

"You're just so damn quiet." Leaning against a tree, I turned my gaze back upward. "I was just thinking about life. I do that a lot when I'm out here."

"Understandable. It's so quiet with no one around to bother you."

I nodded in agreement and then glanced at him. "Well, except for you."

"Ouch." He smirked. "Now that one hurt. I can go away if you'd like?"

"No, you can stay."

He walked over to me and looked up at the stars. "What were you thinking about so intently?"

"The reason I'm always telling you and your team to be careful," I shared.

"What happened?"

I breathed out heavily and hung my head as I remembered that trip to the mountains. We had been in the Rockies, and everything had happened so quickly. It was a miracle no one died.

"I was in charge of a large group like this. We were hiking high in the Rockies. A storm came out of nowhere, and there was a rockslide. One of the younger members of my group got pinned. I stayed with him through the entire thing, holding his hand. Despite all my hoping and praying, I was sure I was going to lose him, but then help finally arrived." I shuddered, remembering when they'd pulled him free. His legs had been so mangled that I'd recognized he'd never walk again.

Josh reached out, placing a hand on my shoulder. "I'm sorry, Trinity, but you don't have to worry so much about us. We'll manage."

I just laughed. "Yeah, I'm kind of realizing that."

I laid my hand over his. His fingers closed around mine as he stepped nearer.

A voice inside my head warned me to take a deep breath and push him away, but my heart was pounding away with excitement. I froze like a deer caught in headlights.

He stepped closer until we were inches from each other. He was a full head taller than me as he stared down into my upturned face. His gaze locked on mine.

"Trinity." He breathed my name like a prayer.

Lost in a sudden wave of arousal, I rose onto my toes and pressed my lips against his soft, warm lips. The kiss deepened quickly, and I imagined I heard him grumble as he folded his arms around me.

I was on fire with a need I'd never felt before. It threw me, but I didn't stop to analyze it.

Josh's hand inched down to grip my hip as

he ground his lower half against mine. I felt his bulge against my stomach as I deepened our kiss.

This was insane.

The searing heat running through my body and the unexplainable impulse to be one with this man was utterly consuming.

When he kissed his way down my neck, I experienced a brief bit of lucidity.

"Stop," I hissed.

"What's wrong?"

"I can't do this," I murmured. "You're a client."

"So?" His hold tightened.

"So let me the fuck go," I demanded.

He nodded before letting go of me and backing away. My knees almost buckled when another wave of need rushed through my body. Dismissing it, I hurried away.

CHAPTER 10
FERGUS

FROM A DISTANCE, we watched Price and the human kissing. I clenched my fists hard, and Cutter whistled.

"Damn, Fergus. She looks like a good fucking kisser. If she survives this, I might have to test her out myself."

I smacked Cutter upside the head. "Stop eye-fucking her, you pervert. We're here to watch Price and his group, not the woman making out with him."

I didn't mention that the second I'd seen them kissing, something black, vile, and vicious reared up inside my head.

Jealousy.

My gut ached as if someone had been kicking it repeatedly.

What the fuck?

This woman meant nothing to me, yet I felt the urge to break cover and rush over to them to smash in Price's fucking teeth.

Grant smirked.

Cutter rubbed the back of his head. "Fine, she's off-limits. So when are we making our move?"

"We have visual confirmation, but you know the rules," I responded.

"Your rules or their rules?" Cutter asked with a lifted eyebrow.

"Mine, you moron. I won't go in until we know for sure she's a member of his pack."

Josh's pack was notoriously traditional and didn't breed with humans like other wolf-shifter packs did.

So what was this human doing with them?

But I had another reason for my rule of waiting before charging in claws first. The one time we'd rushed in after getting a visual of our target, the people had been innocent of the crimes I'd been told they had committed. I'd known we should have waited to watch them actually shift to know for sure if they were what my squad and I hunted.

Never again would I make the same damn error.

Grant nudged me and pointed. "I guess they're done with their foreplay for the night."

I looked on as Price headed back to the fire and the woman vanished into her tent. "Good. Cutter, you have first watch. Wake me up in two hours."

"Yeah, yeah. Whatever you say," Cutter responded dryly.

I growled in warning, sensing Cutter's un-expected need for a fight, but I wasn't in the fucking mood. I needed to get my suddenly frayed thoughts together.

Walking to find a comfortable place in the soil, I sat down beneath a tree and closed my eyes, hoping to have a dreamless sleep, but all I saw was that damn woman's beautiful face.

CHAPTER 11

TRINITY

I CALLED the local park ranger station, which, unfortunately, was nowhere near us and checked in to let them know of my group's progress. We talked for a few minutes to verify my group still had enough supplies and the weather would hold out. I was told the temperature should stay steady, but they'd let me know if it was going to drop drastically. I thanked the park ranger and then hung up.

I held the phone in my hand for a long time before finally deciding I needed to tell somebody about what had happened with Josh.

I dialed Halle's number, knowing I'd likely be yelled at for using the satellite phone for personal reasons, and I waited impatiently for her to pick up.

After five rings, I finally heard her voice come on the line. "Hello?"

"Halle, it's Trinity."

"Hey. Why are you calling? Is something wrong?" She yawned loudly. "You know you're going to get your ass chewed out for using this phone, right?"

"Don't care about that shit right now," I murmured.

"So something is wrong?" Halle asked.

"No, not exactly. Shit, maybe. I don't know," I answered, holding my head. "Damn, I think I might have crossed a line. Now I'm not exactly sure what to do about it." *There.* It was now out in the open.

Silence radiated from the other end before she asked, "Wait, did you sleep with Josh?"

"What? Fuck no—not yet, at least." *Shit, I sounded like some skanky whore.*

Halle laughed. "Oh man, Trinity, breaking your own rules?"

I blew out a breath in frustration. "It's not funny," I argued. "We just kind of made out against a tree a few minutes ago. I'm not even sure why I did it." I really wasn't. Yes, Josh was hot, but he wasn't my type.

"You find him attractive. I don't blame you. He's gorgeous, Trinity."

I wanted to disagree. Something was still bugging me about him. "Can you do me a favor when you get in tomorrow?"

"Sure. What do you need?"

"See what you can dig up on Josh Price. Something about him doesn't seem right."

"Trinity, he passed the background checks. I'm sure he's fine. You're probably just nervous... When was the last time you had sex?"

"Months," I blurted out.

"Exactly. That's the problem. You need some stress relief."

I wanted to quibble with Halle, but I really couldn't. It had been much too long since I'd allowed a man into my body, but I was pretty sure I didn't want to fuck Josh.

"Please just do this for me, Halle."

Another long pause told me she was trying to figure out what was really going on with me.

"Are you in trouble?" she asked. "Because

if you are, I'll have someone fly in and get you out ASAP."

"No, I'm fine. Just check him out for me. Maybe the agency's background investigation missed something. Do some digging into his social life, and as soon as you get anything, call me or let the Alaska park rangers know."

"Will do. I'll see what I can find."

Silence stretched across the line, and then she asked, "Trinity, are you sure you're all right?"

"Yeah," I chirped, trying to sound as if nothing was wrong. All the while, I felt like I was losing my fucking mind. "I'm good. Talk to you soon."

I hung up and lay back on my sleeping bag, trying to relax. My mind kept wandering to how I'd felt while Josh was kissing me. I'd never felt like that before with any man—out of control and desperate to have him in any sexual position he wanted. But it wasn't natural.

Is something compelling me to give Josh what he wants—me?

Besides, Josh was too polished and perfect. Normally, I steered clear of those types of men for good reason. None of them wanted forever. And I was done with one-night stands. However, I was smart enough to know there was no such thing as a white knight who would come in to save me from my loneliness.

After a few minutes, I rolled onto my stomach and buried my head under my pillow.

Sleep—that was what I needed to set my mind right.

We would stay at the campsite for a few nights, and we had little to do except explore the area around us and enjoy the wilderness. Maybe we'd do some swimming in the hot springs. It'd be ungodly cold, but that was exactly what I needed to get my libido under control. A nice icy dip could clear my head and get my heated body back to normal.

CHAPTER 12

FERGUS

I PACED BACK AND FORTH, scanning the campsite. My right eye twitched as it did when I felt my emotions raging out of control.

I don't need this shit.

I couldn't shake the need to charge down into that camp and rip out Price's windpipe. And it wasn't because Price was the target. It was the thought of how he'd been so close to that woman, touching her and kissing her.

My inner bear roared.

The muscles in my shoulders bunched. I'd never felt a primal urge like this before, and it was threatening to tear me apart from the inside out if I didn't do something about it.

Fuck.

The growling in my head started, and I snarled aloud, trying to drown it out. It didn't calm my inner bear. It only pissed him off, making him press against my skin.

He wanted out—to fight, to mate, to claim the human.

Shit, I don't have time for this.

I needed to focus on catching Price and returning him to the facility to pay for his crimes and to help lead us to bigger fish. That was the primary goal of this mission, and I wasn't about to fuck it up because of some woman who had gotten herself caught in the middle of this clusterfuck. She would figure out soon enough who she was dealing with— or kissing under the moonlight. It was no concern of mine.

My bear rumbled with displeasure.

The fire at their campsite died down, and I watched from a distance as, one by one, the others in Price's group turned in for the night, except for one. A lone figure made his way to the woman's tent.

My body tensed, ready to strike.

Boyle.

What is he going to do? Is he going to attack?

He didn't go into her tent, but he stayed outside, crouched low, as if listening to something. I sniffed the air and cursed when I smelled a spike of tension exuding from Boyle that wafted into the air.

Something is wrong.

It took a great deal of effort for me not to lose control right then, but I kept myself calm, breathing deeply as I observed Boyle make his way back through the camp and disappear into another tent.

For whatever reason, Price had brought his group to the wild. I had a feeling I was running out of time to stop whatever he was planning from happening. We'd have to move in closer, and I hoped to bring Josh and his pack down before it was too late.

CHAPTER 13

TRINITY

I WOKE UP EARLY, as I always did, ready to get breakfast going, only to find the fire was already roaring and Price was up along with the rest of the camp. He'd started making breakfast, and his group was sitting around drinking coffee and chatting excitedly with one another. I wondered what had gotten them all in such a chipper mood as I stretched, stifling a yawn.

"Morning," I greeted them, heading over. "What time is it?"

Price winked at me. "Oh, you didn't over-sleep. Don't worry. We all just thought we'd make you breakfast since you've kept us alive this far. Week one is complete, and not a hair is out of place."

"That's nice of you," I replied, sitting down in my camp chair.

The warmth of the fire reached my toes and fingertips as I held them out. It felt nice. I'd been toasty in my tent all night, burrowed deep in my low-temperature sleeping bag and wearing all the essential undergarments for this type of weather. But having a fire was always so much better.

For a few minutes, I just let the fire heat my skin as I inhaled the woodsy scent. Alarm bells started going off in my head, and I opened my eyes to see Josh watching me as intently as he did continually.

"Really," I insisted, clearing my throat at the awkward feeling, "thanks for cooking."

"We don't mind. Besides, today is a big day."

I mentally ran through our itinerary, but nothing came to mind. "And why is that?"

Boyle stalked over with an armful of firewood and leered at me, making me extremely uncomfortable. "It's the anniversary of our company. We've been around for a long time."

"And we plan on being around for a hell of a lot longer," Maggie added loudly.

They all cheered with her, and I felt as if I were missing something.

"That's great," I chimed in, hoping my voice was upbeat enough to cover my suspicions. "Maybe we'll just relax today and play a few games."

"I think we're up for that," Josh exclaimed. "A few rounds of capture the flag?"

"I don't see why not," I responded. "As long as everyone stays fairly close to camp, we should be fine. We haven't seen any bears this whole trip, so we should be safe enough. But that doesn't mean I want anyone to let their guard down. Don't need someone falling off a ridge or into the river."

Everyone nodded in agreement and swore they'd keep an eye out for danger. Josh smirked and met eyes with Boyle. The latter winked before heading off to gather more wood while Josh took a long, hard look into the surrounding trees.

After breakfast, we divided into two teams. Boyle and Josh both gave one of their shirts to be flags, and for the next few hours, I ran around the woods with this interesting group of people.

After we started playing, my thoughts kept going back to the satellite phone in my tent, wondering if Halle had found anything out yet. Something just wasn't sitting well with me about Josh and his group.

Throughout the game, those thoughts kept getting worse. I was on a different team from Josh, and every time I thought I was about ready to sneak around and grab their flag, he'd appear right behind me.

It was eerie how he constantly seemed to know where I was.

One time I swore I heard him sniffing loudly right behind me, and he wasn't the only one. Even if I couldn't see any of the others, somehow they unfailingly found me, sniffing the air, as if it wasn't bizarre to be doing it so noisily. The way they seemed to smell me and follow my trail through the maze of trees was unnerving. No matter how quietly I moved, one would appear around a tree trunk and capture me. I tried to act like it didn't bother me, but they had a predatory look in their eyes every time.

I attempted to brush it off, but when the

game ended, the first thing I did was head to my tent to check the satellite phone.

But when I looked through my bag for it, the phone was gone.

"What the hell?"

I dug through everything, and then I got down on my hands and knees and searched every inch of my tent. It was definitely missing, and so were the other radios I had in case of emergency. Someone had been in my tent.

Heat pumped through my body as I balled my fists tightly.

What the fuck?

Who's gone through my stuff?

Dammit.

What the hell will happen if one of them gets hurt? Help wouldn't be here for hours, maybe even days.

This wasn't a fucking game, and I was tired of them acting like it was.

Pissed, I rushed out of the tent. "Josh!" I yelled.

"What?" he asked, hurrying over to me.

"Someone stole our radios and the satellite phone. Those were our only means of communication in case something happened to one of us," I snapped. "Someone went through my tent to get them."

"Team, get here right now!" he yelled.

Everyone gathered around.

"Who stole the radios?"

Everyone turned to stare at their neighbors and shrugged. No one would fess up, and I wasn't about to stay out in the wilderness with no radio. I might be a thrill seeker, but I wasn't stupid. No radio meant there was no way to call for assistance. If anything went wrong, we were totally alone, miles from anyone who could help.

"This isn't a damn game," I snapped. "Whoever took them needs to hand them over right now. Otherwise, we're turning around and heading to the nearest park ranger station."

None of them moved.

"Okay, this trip is fucking over," I hissed.

"Oh, come on, Trinity. They're just playing a joke." Josh laughed. "We'll find them. I promise."

But I wasn't buying it. "This isn't a joke. I told you this trip needed to be taken seriously. We'll head out first thing in the morning. I suggest you have a talk with your group, Mr.

Price. This is *not* how I run my trips with anyone. No exceptions."

I turned on my heel and stormed off to check on the rest of my supplies. Then I grabbed my canteen to fill with water. When I exited my tent, they were still standing in a huddle, talking too low for me to hear. I didn't give a shit. They could think I was overreacting all they wanted. There was no way in hell I was going to stay out here with someone who thought stealing gear was fun and games.

I headed down to the river, fuming, formulating my plan. I'd take them to the nearest station and demand my bonus, and they could find their own damn way home.

I stayed by the river for a long time, growing angrier when Josh didn't even come to check on me. And I was madder at myself for thinking I needed him to check on me.

On the positive side, at least I'd get to head home sooner. I might take the extra three weeks and go on a vacation for myself. That would be a pleasant change of pace.

CHAPTER 14

FERGUS

STANDING ON THE RIDGELINE, I watched the two bears moving through the woods, heading straight toward me. If anyone else had seen the bears, it would terrify them. It was abnormal to see a grizzly bear traveling side by side with a polar bear.

I lowered my rifle as they approached, and I growled in greeting. The huge polar bear was Grant, and the grizzly was Cutter. Both bowed their heads and grunted back quietly.

"What do you have to report?" I asked.

Both bears took a step back and then stood on their hind legs. Their bones popped and snapped as they changed from large furry beasts into their human forms of Cutter and Grant.

Grant smoothed down his white hair while eyeing me. "Something's happening at the camp. The group cleared out after the woman went down to the river. I think something might have gone wrong."

My body stiffened. "What do you mean?"

"I mean, she yelled at them, something about missing gear. She wasn't happy and looked like she was about to beat the shit out of Price." Cutter smirked. "I wish she had. It would have saved us the trouble of knocking him the fuck out."

I glowered. "Or she would have gotten her hand bitten off. Missing gear?" I arched a brow. "They must have stolen it from her. I'm getting the feeling she's not part of the reason we're after Price."

Cutter and Grant nodded in agreement.

"From the way they acted," Grant added, "they were furious about her yelling. It showed disrespect, if she were one of them."

I concurred with his assessment. "No matter. We'll move in tonight."

Cutter glanced at me with a tilted head. "What's wrong?"

"What do you mean?" I replied.

"I can smell your uneasiness. Is it about the woman?"

I glared at him, even as my inner bear whined obnoxiously in my head. The whining grew louder until I winced, fighting the urge to hold my head. Mercifully, after a while, it died down. I took a deep breath in through my nostrils, hoping the other two wouldn't notice, but from their wide-eyed stares, I knew they had.

"No, it has nothing to do with the human," I snapped. "Why do you ask?"

"Fuck, bro." Grant grabbed his bundle of clothes. "No need to get all ornery. It was just a question." He strode away without a backward glance.

Cutter snatched his clothes too.

Grant was right. I was acting like a snappy asshole.

"Shit. I meant nothing by it."

"We just worry about you sometimes."

I glanced at Grant's back and then at Cutter. "Meaning what?"

"Meaning you're at your prime to find a mate, and you have yet to seek one out. The clan's worried about you, especially your aunt

Kristine. We all just want to make sure your alpha bloodline continues and the clan remains strong."

"Well, you all need to mind your own damn business," I snapped. "Get back to your positions. We'll move in soon enough."

Cutter stared at me long and hard until I snarled, "I'm fine, Cutter."

He raised a brow and replied, "Sure you are." He took a long sniff of the air. "Do you smell that?"

I barely moved my head in acknowledgment as I stepped toward the south. The scent was there, just a hint in the wind. A herd of elk was moving through the area, close to where we stood. I hadn't eaten all day, and neither had Cutter and Grant.

A snarl echoed around my head, and my teeth snapped in response. "Let's go," I told Cutter. "Before we take out Price and his group, we should let our beasts feed."

Cutter grinned darkly and sprinted away after Grant, shifting mid run. Then a large grizzly bear was lumbering through the trees.

Quickly, I removed my gear, stripping out of my clothes. The air was chilly as the sun was going down, but I barely felt the change in temperature. My skin was naturally warm from the beast raging within me.

As I stepped forward, the shift took over my body. A shooting pain raced through me as my inner beast rushed forth. Bones rearranged under my skin, expanding and stretching. The fur grew, covering my entire body, as my feet and hands spread and thickened. A few snaps of ribs later and a monstrous grizzly stood in my place, roaring in the night.

My dark chestnut fur rippled down my body in waves. Along my back were streaks of golden fur, a trademark of my bloodline, marking me as the alpha male of my clan. It was a position I had taken seriously for nearly ten years. When my uncle had passed, I had taken part in the contest to become alpha, and I'd won over the rest of the males in my family. Since that night, I'd led my clan with a firm hand. The position was challenging but rewarding.

As bear-shifters, we were notoriously territorial and loners. We preferred to live in isolation from others, but bear-shifters were diminishing because of the females having breeding problems and wars with wolf-shifters over territory. So now it wasn't un-common for bear-shifters to live in clans under the leadership of an alpha to ensure the survival of our species.

Just a few years back, a run-in with hu-mans had shown me how precarious our lives were. A soldier had captured a member of my clan near a military base in the mountains. The soldiers hadn't known what to do with the man, who had been a bear only moments before. The clan had been in an uproar and ready to charge the base to get our brother back. However, I'd sworn to get him back peacefully, if possible.

I had gone to the base, walking right up to the main road as a bear. As I'd gotten closer, I'd shifted into a naked man. At first, the sol-diers had been prepared to shoot me, but the man in charge, General Harry Taggert, had stopped them. He'd come out against the protests of his men and greeted me.

Together, we'd come to an arrangement that only men on that base would know about.

With Cutter, who was my second-in-com-mand and beta, and Grant, who was my head enforcer, we had become part of a special task force, a band of brothers, completing missions for the US government under the most top secret conditions they could manage. General Taggert had sworn to keep our existence confidential, and he'd released my clan member.

Ever since then, I'd been going to the base every few weeks. My clan didn't trust the general even though I did.

In the beginning, I'd worried he'd go back on his word. I'd feared the government would raid my clan's lands, take my family away for dissection. But General Taggert never revealed to anyone that he had shifters working for him.

In the end, he'd turned out to be very trustworthy.

He'd even accepted an invitation to come to my home for dinner and meet a few clan members. Several of the cheekier clan members had tried to scare the general off, but he'd only laughed. He'd told them I was the only shifter he feared.

As two powerful leaders, we'd built a trust over the years. We had tested our trust many times, but it had yet to break under the strain of secrecy.

My small team, Cutter and Grant, had been on over one hundred special missions, bringing in dangerous enemies, threats to the government and the country. In the beginning, we'd dealt solely with human targets because Taggert hadn't known about the bigger threat—feral and rogue shifters who refused to abide by the shifter code of conduct.

Then one day General Taggert had called me and started asking questions about the existing number of bear-shifter clans and wolf-shifter packs. His questions made me uncomfortable. It was one thing to reveal the existence of my clan but quite another to out other shifters.

I was a member of the Shifter Council—a secretive group of alpha leaders from various shifter breeds—and sworn to secrecy.

So I'd compromised, giving him a number of rogue wolf-shifter packs that had become a nuisance to other shifters because of their reckless behavior of killing shifters and humans. But that was all the information I'd been willing to provide him.

That was a few years ago, and soon after that first meeting, Josh Price had shown up on General Taggert's radar.

I'd already known about Price. Most shifters did. He was an alpha of a rogue wolf-shifter pack. Price showed little respect to other shifters and had flat out refused to abide by shifter law mandated by the council. The world was dangerous for shifters. Humans could discover our existence if we didn't follow the laws that governed our conduct.

But Price felt he was above shifter law. Rumors had said Price was ruthless and ruled his pack by intimidation. When he'd become the alpha of his pack, he'd murdered quite a few males who he'd thought could challenge him for the alpha position.

When he'd shown up on General Taggert's radar, Josh had been busy making a name for himself in many circles and not in a good way. The local police had been cleaning up bodies, and they still did not know where they'd come from. The corpses were mutilated, and all the reports had pointed to the same cause of death—wild animal attacks.

But I'd known what was really going on, and my team and I were under orders to bring in Price and as many of his group, alive, as we could.

Seven against three wasn't bad odds, and I was always up for a challenge.

I ran through the trees, my big black

nose sniffing the wind. Elk were definitely nearby, and my bear growled in anticipation of the kill. I had cooped up my inner beast for the past week while tracking Price. It was easier to hide as a man than as a giant grizzly bear, especially when Grant was a polar bear. That wouldn't be easy to explain away at all.

I caught up to Cutter and Grant, standing taller than both of them, as they waited for orders. I shook out my head and motioned for them to get a move on toward the elk.

We had just turned to head down to the valley floor when another scent hit my nose, and I stood on my hind legs, snarling.

Wolves, I grumbled through the mental link all shifters shared with their clans or packs.

Grant and Cutter stopped beside me.

It's Price and his pack. They've shifted, I explained.

Do we move in? Cutter asked. His bear growled and snapped his teeth, biting at the wind. As usual, he wanted a fight.

We don't have a choice. I fell back down to all fours and hurried through the woods.

Taggert had charged us with finding

Price, but there was another reason we'd tracked them this far north.

This was my territory.

Price in human form was fine on the land, but the second he'd shifted, he'd broken shifter law. I was now forced to act before Price could spill the blood of an innocent in my territory. Hunting animals was one thing —still disrespectful, but not against shifter law. If Josh spilled a human's blood, like the human woman's, I wouldn't be taking him in alive. I'd have to kill him and the pack members he'd dragged with him.

I sighed heavily. I had a nuclear option for dealing with Josh and his pack before they hurt the human. I could call my contact Travis, the leader of the Protectors. Their organization was made up of hybrids born with a distinctive mark, shifter-like fighting, tracking, and hunting skills but with no ability to transform into shifters. After all, it was the Protectors' job to protect humans from shifters.

But calling the Protectors could subject me to questions that I didn't want to answer, like how I knew so much about Josh and his pack and the human. And I couldn't let anyone outside my clan know we worked for the government or that Taggert had charged us with finding Price.

No. Price was our mission, and we'd never failed.

It was best to stay off the Protectors' radar.

When we reached the end of the valley, I shifted back to my human form and crouched low in the brush, trying to find Price and the others. The herd of elk was moving through the open field. My bear growled loudly in my mind, but I silenced him. There wasn't time to let my instincts take over—at least not yet.

I had to bring in Price—still breathing. Otherwise, I'd have a lot more explaining to do with General Taggert.

I whiffed the breeze again and bent my head to the west. As I watched, I saw glowing eyes appear at the edge of the trees. My fingers turned to claws as they dug into the bark of a nearby tree, my beast growing angry at the sight of intruders in my territory.

They were all wolves. *But where is the woman?*

I heard footsteps crunch behind me. Then a growl turned into a human groan as Cutter came up beside me.

"Do we move in yet?" he asked.

"No, we'll watch them. I don't want this to get messier than it has to be. This is our territory they're in. I'm hoping they know better."

"What about the woman?"

I wasn't going to charge in prematurely and risk my team for some stupid human. "She'll eventually find out who they are. Then maybe she'll get away."

"And if not?"

"We'll wait," I proclaimed, not bothering to answer the question directly.

What will I do if the woman doesn't realize who she's with? Will I step in and save her?

I'd caught her kissing Price, but that didn't mean she knew what she'd become involved with.

From this distance, I couldn't see much, but I knew she wasn't with them in the trees. I peeked back to where their camp was, and my muscles clenched involuntarily. I had a sudden urge to run to her and protect her.

I don't care about her. She's only a human.

"Fergus?" Cutter's voice pulled me out of my sudden daze.

I straightened. "Wait for my order to move in. Understand?"

Cutter nodded as I continued to watch the wolves at the edge of the trees, ready for them to make their move.

CHAPTER 15
TRINITY

AFTER MY CONFRONTATION WITH PRICE, I went to my tent, intending to stay there for the rest of the day, but then he came by and asked, "Do you want dinner?"

Ignoring his question, I asked, "Did you figure out what happened to the gear?"

"You're the guide. Are you sure you even packed it?" he retorted.

My mouth tightened. "Go shove your fucking dinner up your damn ass."

When he walked away after trying to reason with me but failing, I lay back in my sleeping bag and gazed at the tent roof. I refused to speak with any of them until the next morning. When the sun came up, I'd be moving out—with or without them.

I had seen something in Josh's eyes when I'd asked him about the radio for the first time. He'd lied to me. I wasn't sure why, but I could sense it.

And if he lied about that, what else has he not told the truth about?

And why did he take my communication devices?

For most of the daytime, I could hear them running around the camp, but at sunset, it became quiet. I paced back and forth inside my tent, wondering what I was going to do. Then I decided I couldn't take it anymore. I grabbed my pocketknife, tucked it into my pants pocket, unzipped my tent, and then peeked out.

The campsite was empty. They had built up a large fire, and the huge flames reached nearly ten feet into the air.

What are they trying to do? Burn down the tents?

I rushed toward it and threw handfuls of dirt onto the logs to tamp down the hungry flames before they ignited the forest.

"Fucking idiots. Where did they go?" I

mumbled, glaring around the empty site. *So help me God, if they get lost out here, I'm not sticking around to find their sorry asses.*

I couldn't hear them, and I didn't see a trail leading into the woods. There was no sign of them. It was as though they'd just up and disappeared.

Since the campsite was empty, I wasn't about to lose this chance to search for the radios and satellite phone. Josh had refused to do it, so he'd left me with no other option but to take care of it myself. I had no issues with going through people's things. Growing up in foster homes, I'd learned there was no such thing as privacy, especially when it came to having anything of my own.

I started with Boyle and Owen's tent, but I found nothing, so I moved on to Ian and Brian's tent nearby, and it was the same deal. I took a long glance around the campsite again before I unzipped Maggie and Brenda's tent and slipped inside. There was nothing in their tent either, but it smelled funny, musky.

"God, what is that wicked smell?" I wrinkled my nose. After taking a quick peek around, I left and went inside Josh's tent.

In the middle of it was a pile of blankets,

almost like a nest. *Does he sleep curled up like that?*

I stepped closer, the musky smell almost overpowering me in there, and gazed down at the covers that were caked in black hair. The longer I stared at it, the more I realized it looked like dog fur. Halle had a large black dog, and her couch always looked like this. But Josh didn't have a dog with him.

I shook my head and kept up my hunt. I didn't have time for more questions. All I wanted was the damn satellite phone so I could call for the helicopter to come get me.

Josh's duffel was in the corner, and I rapidly poked through it. It didn't take long before I found the satellite phone and the radios buried underneath his clothes.

"What the hell? You bastard!" I yelled, pulling out the satellite phone.

I immediately dialed the local park ranger station. It took a few rings before someone finally answered.

"Yes, this is Trinity Holiday. I'm the guide with Josh Price's group. I need you to—"

The phone was ripped out of my hand.

"What the fuck?" I yelled.

Multiple hands reached into the tent and

yanked me out by my shoulders and hair. My scalp erupted in pain, and the fingers on my shoulders dug in deep, nearly smashing the bone.

"Oh hell no. Get the hell off me."

They dropped me to the earth. When I glanced up, I found Josh and the rest of them glaring down at me. Josh held the satellite phone in his hands, and I watched as he crushed it to pieces, sprinkling them onto the ground in front of me.

I sat up and stared at the pieces and then back to Josh. "Who the fuck are you?"

"Were you trying to leave us, Trinity?" he asked darkly, a growl under his words.

I tried to get to my feet, but Boyle shoved me back down.

"What are you doing? What is this shit? You can't keep me here!" I screamed, one step away from passing out.

"Oh, Trinity," Josh crooned as he crouched down, running his fingers over my forehead.

I was too stunned to move away.

"You are the chosen one," he told me. "So special in so many ways, and you have no idea."

I glared at him. *What is going on? Are they part of a cult?*

"First, I'm not a virgin, so if you want to sacrifice me for some weird ritual, it won't work." Josh glowered at my words, but I rambled on. "And second, I don't care what you guys are into. I will not be a part of it. I'm going to grab my gear, head to the park ranger station, and get my ass home. You all can stay out here and be crazy on your own time."

I attempted to move again, but Boyle wouldn't let me.

"Get your hands off me, you asshole."

"She has some fight in her." Boyle laughed, barely using any effort to keep me in place. "It's going to be a fun run this year, Alpha."

"Alpha? Are you kidding me?" I shrieked, relieved that he'd eased his hold, allowing me to get onto my knees.

"Be quiet," Maggie snarled. She lunged forward, making me fall backward. "Show respect, you filthy human."

I got back to my knees, trying to keep my fear in check even as I shook. "Human? We are all humans, you crazy bitch."

I gazed around at them with wide eyes as everything slowly snapped into place.

But that's impossible. There's no way... Just—no!

But I'd seen their eyes, the way they'd hunted, the way they'd tracked me.

Holy fucking shit. I felt my mind closing down.

"It's time. Bring her," Josh demanded before turning.

He walked away into the trees, and the rest of the group followed. Boyle seized my upper arm and yanked me to my feet. He dragged me along even as I tried to dig in my heels.

If they were going to kill me or sacrifice me or whatever, I wasn't about to go down easy. I fought against Boyle's grip until he finally became annoyed. He hauled off and smacked me across the face. It stung. I floundered and lost my balance, but Boyle didn't give me a chance to recuperate.

He pulled me along through the trees, but I didn't give up fighting. I clawed with everything I had, even threatened to bite him, when he raised his hand to strike me again. But a harsh growl from Josh in front of the group stayed Boyle's hand.

I hadn't even noticed we'd come to a stop at the edge of the trees. Josh held up his hand, and the rest fell in beside him. Boyle dragged me to him, and Josh took hold of my other arm and twisted my face so I stared down into the duskiness of the vale.

"What are we looking at?" I snarled. "Are you going to throw me down there or something?"

"No, Trinity, you will not die—at least not yet."

"Oh thanks. That's comforting," I grumbled.

He gripped my jaw harder and turned my back to the valley.

"I can't see anything. It's too dark. Just tell me already."

"Elk, an entire herd of them!" he shouted.

I shivered at the carnal tone of his words but kept a brave face. "Great. Can I go home now?"

He pinched my cheek, making me wince.

"You're going to watch and see what you humans are too blind to see about your own world," Josh growled. "Tie her up."

"No. Let me go."

Boyle and Owen snatched me and pulled me back to a tree. They wrapped a rope tightly around my upper body, pressing me back into the bark. I struggled to get loose, but it was taut.

I'm trapped.

I felt the biting cold of the night seeping deeper into my bones.

After a few minutes, I wasn't sure if I was shivering from the cold or from fear.

Josh stalked over to me and grinned. "You will watch, and then you will understand."

"Understand what? That you guys are all psychos?"

Josh laughed darkly and then took a step back from me until he stood in line with the rest of them. Then they all stripped nude.

Shit. Shit. Shit. I am in real fucking trouble. This is some freaky satanic ritual, and I'm the sacrifice.

He said nothing, but he bent his gaze upward toward the night sky. He shut his eyes, and a tremor ran down the length of his torso. I watched, transfixed, praying he was having a fucking seizure and would just drop dead, but what happened next made me curse and try even harder to get away.

Josh fell to all fours as his body became covered in black fur, while loud snaps and popping filled my ears. His head transformed into that of a wolf, and he snarled at me, flashing sharp canines. He was tall at the shoulders with enormous paws, and for a second, I thought I was daydreaming.

Josh threw his wolf's head back and howled. It sent chills racing down my spine, and I finally realized why I'd always felt the need to run away when I was near him.

He was a fucking werewolf. This crap rated a 9.5 on my shit-o-meter.

I stared at him, amazed, despite the fear threatening to make me black out. The rest of them changed as well, shifting into massive killer beasts. Price was a black wolf, Boyle a black wolf with a long, jagged scar running along his face, Ian a silver wolf, Owen a brown-and-black wolf, Brian's fur was sand, Maggie's white with black variations, and Brenda had blond fur.

They stalked toward me, growling and nipping at one another, until the wolf that was Josh howled again. He darted off, down to the valley floor, and the rest of them followed. From where I was, I could see them until they disappeared for just a moment before they popped back up near a herd of elk.

I was still in shock at what was taking place before my eyes.

It wasn't possible.

It couldn't be.

Yet there they were.

Seven humans had just turned into wolves—big, furry, probably-going-to-eat-me-later wolves.

How the hell did I get trapped in this bloody nightmare?

The satellite phone was broken, but the radios were still in the tent. All I had to do was get back there and contact someone, any-one, to come rescue me. Maybe, while they were busy, I'd be able to sneak off... But when I looked back toward the valley floor, I found I couldn't look away. Their bodies moved as one through the tall grass, downwind from the elk. The poor creatures did not know what was coming toward them.

Part of me wanted to scream out, but that would probably just piss off Josh. And dealing with him in this wolf form wasn't something I could handle. For all I knew, he'd just rip me apart with his claws.

Frankly, I wasn't sure why I was still alive.

Why did they reveal themselves to me?

In fact, why the hell did they bring me out here at all?

None of it made sense. I wasn't anyone special. There was nothing unique about me that should draw the attention of something supernatural.

The wolves moved in closer, and the moment the elk raised their heads and ran, the pack lunged forward to attack. They moved in from two different angles and singled out a large elk.

Josh leaped forward, landing on the elk's back with a growl I heard from the top of the ridge. The elk screamed as Josh took it down. Then the other wolves moved in for the killing blow. They ripped the elk's throat out with one of their sharp canines, and blood spurted into the air. The scene before me was revolting, but I still couldn't look away.

As the rest of the herd raced off, they left me with the sounds of the dying elk, followed by the howls of the wolf pack. They tilted their heads back as one and let their voices carry through the wild.

"Jesus fucking Christ," I whispered.

Then I waited as they worked their way back upward to me, dragging the bleeding, broken elk body behind them.

CHAPTER 16
FERGUS

WELL, that answers that question, Cutter rumbled through our mental link as Grant and I stood beside him. *Don't think she knew what they were.*

Apparently not, I replied tightly as my right eye twitched.

I growled, seeing the woman tied to a tree as she had been forced to watch Price and the rest of his small group shift right before her eyes. Then they had gone hunting, and even from this distance, I could smell the fear pouring off her, not that I could blame her. I could only imagine what was going through her head right then. She was lucky there weren't any other shifters around besides my group and Price's.

If anyone else had smelled her fear, it would draw them straight to her.

Stupid humans.

Fearful of what they don't understand.

My bear whined and pawed anxiously at the ground. I was torn between what I usually felt for humans and this woman, this insane woman who had found herself alone in the wilderness with a pack of shifters.

Do we move in? Grant asked, yanking me from my thoughts.

No, we'll wait. I don't want to risk this chance of catching Price, I responded.

Price had killed an elk in our territory. Technically, that wasn't against shifter law, but if they shifted in front of a human un-aware of shifters, killed the woman, or hurt her, then I would have a vendetta against Price and his entire pack—not just those here, but any he might have left behind in my terri-tory. It would start a war, something that hadn't happened between the shifters in decades, and I didn't have time to deal with that.

But if Price started it, I would be the one to finish it, no questions asked.

Cutter, Grant, keep a close watch on the campsite, I ordered. *I'm going to call home base and see if Taggert has any new information.*

Might want to check back home, too, Grant suggested. *Just in case things go south.*

Let's hope they don't, I replied.

I made my way back through the trees. When I reached my gear, I shifted back into my six-foot-three human form and pulled on my gear. I tried to ignore the whining of my bear in my head. I kept thinking back to the woman and the fear on her face as she'd watched the wolves hunt and take down the elk.

Part of me wanted to run to her, rip the ropes off her body, and take her far away from here, from this nightmare.

But she was a human. I should have no feelings for her.

So why won't the beast inside me shut up?

It was acting as if she were my fated mate.

Oh fuck no. There's no way that's happening. I was the alpha of the largest bear-shifter clan in Alaska and destined to mate with an alpha-female shifter.

I ignored the inner beast, reaching my gear where I could get some sort of signal to call Taggert and then check in back home with the clan.

My home was near Valdez, out in the Alaskan wilderness, where my family could roam freely without the fear of being spotted by humans. My family's territory, which had been passed on to me when my parents died, was vast and had grown over the years by acquiring property via the annual sealed-bid land auctions. But it was getting harder to keep up with the needs of my clan and the demands of my position on the council. Plus there was always a lot of pressure on me to keep the peace with other shifters, especially the wolves. For centuries, there had been territory disputes, but for the past fifty years, peace had reigned between the families.

I wondered how long it was going to last. Price had to know he was in bear territory.

So why risk coming out here to hunt?

Not to mention, why did he bring a human if they are trying to keep the peace?

I radioed home base and told the man at

the other end to connect me to Taggert. The soldier told me to hold on for a minute while he figured out where the general was. I waited impatiently as my bear clawed at the edges of my mind, begging to come out and go to the woman. The struggle made my head pound. It took everything I had to fight the instinctual need tearing up my gut.

That damn woman.

If it weren't for her, this mission would likely be over.

I needed to keep it together. *Maybe it's been too long since I had a good roll in the woods with another bear. Yes, that's exactly what it is.*

"Sheenan? Did you get Price yet?" General Taggert's voice came over the satellite phone.

"Not yet, sir, but we currently have eyes on him and his wolves."

"Why haven't you moved in yet? It's been over a week since I sent you out there."

I chewed my cheek for a second. I had to be careful how I played this. Not that I didn't trust General Taggert. I just didn't want to give away too much information about my kind and how we worked outside the laws of the formal government.

"We've run into a bit of a problem. I'm figuring out how best to deal with it."

For a long minute, there was quiet before General Taggert's rough voice came back along the communication channel. "Fine, deal with it however you have to, but I want this wrapped up sooner rather than later. Understood?"

"Yes, sir."

"So if you don't have Price in custody, why did you call?"

"Do you have any new information on Price? Maybe something that would explain a few more things about him?"

"Hmm, let me check," General Taggert mumbled. I heard some papers being shuffled in the background, and he cleared his throat. "Actually, we do. We finally got permission to search his land in Nebraska, and... Well, let's just say we found more than we'd bargained for."

I felt a tightness in my chest. "Meaning what, sir?"

"We dug up a damn graveyard, that's what. Bodies everywhere, lots of them.

There's no record of a cemetery ever being there and no sign of tombstones. They're still searching to see how many bodies there actually are. But," he added, "we heard something interesting from our pathology experts."

I really hated when he did this—dragged out our conversations instead of just giving me what I needed. It was one of the general's tactics to get me to let something slip. I always had to be on guard when I talked to the damn man.

"And what's that?" I asked.

"Using forensic entomology—"

I cut him off. "What is forensic entomology?"

"It's a new field in the study of forensics that helps examiners determine the time of death by looking at insect activity on a body. Different types and stages of bugs found on or inside a body can help narrow down the time of death."

"Okay, got it. Continue," I encouraged him.

"Using forensic entomology—insect activity—my experts determined the kills were a year apart from each other, at least the ones they've been able to check out so far. Strange, don't you think?"

More than just a question was in his tone, but I ignored it. My mind was too busy racing with the realization that this woman was in far more trouble than I'd originally thought. Killing her was one thing, but if the people were killed about one year apart...

Oh fuck no. Is that what Price is doing all the way up here?

"The Hunt," I hissed aloud.

Centuries ago, the Shifter Council had outlawed the Hunt. They punished any shifter caught taking part in such a barbaric act with death.

According to shifter elders, the Hunt started eons ago as a pack ritual for the right of becoming the second—the alpha was the first—strongest hunter-warrior in the pack. First, the alpha chose a human as prey for the Hunt. Second, the alpha presented the human prey to the pack. Third, the alpha released the human on the night of the full moon and ordered the pack to give chase—the Hunt. The alpha ran down the prey with his pack but gave the honor of killing the human to the pack. The member who killed the human got the privilege of eating their heart under the full moon. They recognized that shifter as the second-strongest hunter-warrior of the pack until the next Hunt.

"What was that?" Taggert asked.

"Nothing, sir. Must have been static. If that's all, then I'll be signing off. I need to check with my men."

I waited for General Taggert to either argue with me or let it go, and thankfully, he was too tired to care or assumed I would fill him in later.

"Fine. But I want a full report when we detain Price."

"Yes, sir," I replied. Then I ended the call before the general could ask anything else.

Pacing back and forth, I watched distant clouds roll in over the treetops. It was getting colder. The National Weather Service called for the temperature to drop and maybe even a bit of snow. It wasn't uncommon this time of year.

The bear in me growled in pleasure at the thought of snowflakes hitting my face, and then he immediately snarled when I recalled my conversation with General Taggert.

The Hunt.

It had been a long-standing tradition with shifters until the moral-minded Shifter Council had put an end to it. It was against shifter law and punishable by death if committed.

And here Price and his pack had been continuing the ritual every single damn year. That was why they were in the Alaskan wilderness. It made sense. Price thought they were safe and could hide from the system. And he might have succeeded, too, if I had never become a part of General Taggert's team of special operatives.

I was in a tough spot. By shifter law, I could punish the wolves by killing them and sending their heads home as a warning to the rest of Price's pack. Technically, his pack couldn't retaliate, but that didn't mean they wouldn't try.

And Josh's pack was large. He had family all across the Midwest, and I knew if I spilled one drop of wolf blood, they'd all come running. Wolves were loyal to their pack members. They'd go on and on about revenge and serving out judgment. It gave other shifter breeds headaches just listening to wolf-shifters bellyache about past slights.

I didn't even want to think about what Price's untimely death would bring out of the woodwork. All shifters were a bit on the crazy side, but wolf-shifters were the true psychos of the shifter breed.

I called another number and waited for it to be answered. The minute it did, the sounds on the other end brought a grin to my face, warming my spirit.

"Fergus? Why are you calling? Is everything all right?" my aunt Kristine asked.

The woman might be nearly three hundred years old, but she still sounded young. She was the caretaker for the young bear-shifters when their parents were away on clan business. She told stories to keep our heritage alive in the younger generations, making us remember where we'd come from.

I shuddered because I wouldn't know what to do if I ever lost her, especially if we began a war with the wolf-shifters.

Pushing the dark thought aside, I responded, "Can you put Logan on the phone?"

"I haven't seen Logan in a week."

I frowned. Logan should have been home by now. He was one of my newest enforcers and eager to prove himself to the clan, so I'd sent him to Price's territory to do surveillance. All shifters spied on one another. It wasn't a secret. It was how we kept one another in check.

"Has there been any news of wolf-shifters on the move?" I asked.

"Wolves, eh? Not that I'm aware of..." She paused. "Wait, why are you asking about wolves, Fergus? And don't lie to me."

"I wouldn't dream of it, but I can't get into details."

"Hmm, well, I have heard more grumbling about that unruly Price pack. They found some more mutilated animal bodies a couple of states over, and I hear humans are now getting very suspicious."

Shit. I ran my fingers through my hair. "Have you heard about anything strange happening in his territory?"

Screaming children in the background had my aunt yelling, "If you don't settle down, there will be no honeycomb cookies for dessert!"

Then there was utter silence.

"No. Nothing like that, Fergus." She sighed into the phone before asking, "What's troubling you? You sound upset by something."

I leaned against a nearby tree as a few gentle snowflakes fell around me. They landed on my warm skin and melted instantly.

"The Hunt," I whispered, as if afraid someone would overhear me. For a second, I felt like a damn little kid asking why curse words were bad and then being smacked on the knuckles for uttering them all out loud.

And my aunt's reaction was just the same. I heard a sharp intake of breath and then the sound of a door slamming shut.

"Why do you speak about such dreadful things?"

"Because I believe it's still going on, Aunt Kristine. And I think I just found their next victim."

CHAPTER 17

TRINITY

I WAS STILL in shock when Boyle and Josh changed back into men. The rest stayed as they were, dragging the dead elk between them.

Josh untied me and then shoved me ahead of him as we headed back to camp.

My hands curled into tight fists. "If you fucking shove me again, I'm going to kick your ass," I snapped.

He looked at my fists and just smiled, as if he'd love to see me try.

If it wasn't because he was an animal, I would've taken my chances and fought for my freedom. But the horrific scene I'd witnessed with them taking down that elk had proven I was no match for their animal side.

I moved numbly, stumbling every few steps, as my mind tried to understand what had happened. Josh and his group weren't human. But my rational mind rejected the possibility. That shit just wasn't conceivable.

In fact, any second, I was going to wake up and realize this whole damn day had been a nightmare.

Then I faltered, fell, and hit my knee on a rock. It hurt like hell as the pain zinged up my leg.

"Shit!" I yelled as blood welled up in the rip of my cargo pants. "Dammit," I snapped.

Josh yanked me backward onto my feet.

"Can you give me a fucking second?"

He snarled. "No. Keep moving. We have a feast to get on with," he barked. "And you're going to watch."

I wanted to punch him in the damn face, but he seemed like the type of man who would actually enjoy the pain.

"You can't force my eyes to remain open," I argued as we reached the campsite.

Boyle built the fire back up, hot as it had

been before I'd gotten caught going through Josh's tent.

"I won't watch." My eyes narrowed.

Josh laughed as he shoved me forward, and I fell again with a curse.

"Yes, you will. You stand before one of the oldest shifter packs in the world, Trinity, and you will watch in awe at our strength, our beauty, and especially our hunger."

I grinned for a second and then spat in his face. "Fuck off."

The other wolves were on me instantly. They pushed me flat onto my back in the mud. Their snapping teeth were inches from my face; their foul breath smelled of blood and death. It filled my nose, making me gag at the rotten stench. Drool fell from their mouths and landed on my skin. It was hot and disgusting, but I was too busy watching their sharp teeth to be bothered by drops of spit.

"Enough. Leave her be," Josh thundered.

The wolves reluctantly backed up, then disappeared into the darkness.

Scrambling, I quickly sat up, backing away as far as I could until my back hit a tree. My heart thudded in my chest. My palms were sweaty, but I didn't flinch when Josh came toward me, still naked from head to toe.

His shaft was long and erect as he leaned in. He wrapped a hand around my neck, pulling my face up to meet his. I didn't brace myself before he pressed his lips against mine, trying to force his tongue into my mouth. Stubbornly, I refused to allow him entry, pressing my teeth together. He just laughed before licking my lips. I bit his lip to get him to back off and shoved against his chest.

"Damn," he yelled. Then he smacked me across the cheek.

I winced from the sting but kept quiet, refusing to give him the satisfaction of crying out.

"Fine, Trinity. Have it your way. I was going to let you enjoy a little more fun before the full moon tomorrow night, but you don't appreciate my graciousness."

As he walked away, he nodded at Boyle, who came over, rope in hand, and yanked me to my feet.

He forced my arms down to my sides, then looped the rope around my body and the tree. I wriggled against the ropes, but Boyle had made them so stiff that I struggled to move my upper body or arms. It would be hard as hell to escape, but I was determined to do so.

"What the hell are you?" I snarled. If I was going to die, I fucking wanted to know why. "Werewolves?"

Josh grumbled, "We are wolf-shifters. Werewolf was a name given to us by weak humans. It's an insult. Shifters own the night and the day."

I glanced behind him as the wolves pulled the elk all the way into camp, but none of them changed back to their human forms to eat.

I shuddered. *Are they going to eat it like that?*

"So what does that mean?" I needed to keep him talking. Just standing there, listening to the wolves tear into the elk, made me sick. Talking would help keep me focused on something else.

"It means you have the honor of being in our presence. I'm over three hundred years old. Boyle here is my second-in-command and just a few years younger. He's repeatedly proven his merit, fighting by my side. The others with me are very important members of my pack. This isn't just a vacation for us. It is something so much greater than that."

Boyle grinned darkly as he stepped closer and licked his lips. I watched him shift back into the giant black wolf I'd seen earlier. The scar he had as a human was even more terrifying on his wolf's face. I fought against the ropes as he stalked forward, snarling and biting into the air. I tried not to scream, but I couldn't stop the noise from bubbling up my throat and spewing loudly out of my mouth.

"Down, Boyle." Josh leered. "There will be time for that on the full moon if you win. Now, let's eat."

Boyle turned and joined the rest of the wolves at the elk carcass.

Josh winked at me as I stared in horror. He shifted again, and with a loud howl, he dug into the elk flesh, ripping and tearing it apart into a bloody mess. I attempted to tune out the cracking bones and their guttural growls as they ate as one. It was revolting.

When I did glance over, I froze. There, beneath their jaws, was a vision of my lifeless body. I shuddered, and the elk reappeared under their chomping mouths, but the image stuck with me.

Are they going to eat me next?

CHAPTER 18
FERGUS

I MADE my way back to Grant and Cutter, ordering them to shift back to their human forms. The two men stood before me, snowflakes falling on their naked shoulders as they bowed their heads in respect to me, their alpha.

"So what did you find out?" Cutter asked.

"Not good news," I reported. "How's the woman? Still alive?" I'd tried to fight it, but the words had come out before I could stop them. My inner bear was the one who had demanded I ask the question.

Grant glanced sideways at Cutter before answering, "She's alive, bound to a tree, and breathing."

"Good. We need to move fast. She might not be alive for long."

"What do you mean?" Cutter demanded.

I stared at him. "The wolves, it seems, are still honoring the yearly Hunt, and the woman is their next victim."

"You've got to be shitting me." Cutter laughed. "If the Protectors get wind that they're trying to revive that antiquated, barbaric tradition, they'll kill every one of them. There's no way they're that stupid!"

"They're wolves," Grant added with disgust written all over his face.

Cutter shook his head. "Yeah, but to come to another clan's territory and then try to perform a Hunt? Is he trying to start a war?"

"I don't know, but the second it starts or when they kill her, I'll have no choice but to step in and take care of things our way."

"What will you tell Taggert?" Grant asked.

I sighed at his question. "I'll figure it out when the time comes. For now, we move in. If they're feeding, we might catch them off guard. Let's go."

I yawned, which turned into a roar as I released my beast. Snow fell onto my fur and melted, cooling me in little bursts of chill. I peeked over my big shoulder as Cutter and Grant shifted.

Together, we made our way back through the woods to stop a bloody shifter war before it could start.

CHAPTER 19

TRINITY

THEIR FEEDING WAS GETTING to me. I couldn't drown it out any longer, and I knew the second I opened my eyes, I'd puke. I didn't have a weak stomach, but listening to them munching away on a corpse just feet from me was nauseating. Bile rose in my throat, and I tried to swallow it back down.

After a few deep breaths, I was all right until Boyle turned his wolf's head toward me. His snout was covered with blood, and something was dangling from his teeth. It seemed to be a part of an intestine.

I turned my head seconds before everything came up. I heaved and coughed, getting it all out, even as I heard a man's laughter over my groaning.

Josh had shifted back to human form. "Oh, Trinity. You humans are so pathetic," he raged.

He glared as I spat up more vomit, and then I took a deep breath. It was a bad idea. He reeked of death and blood and some other bodily fluids I really didn't want to think about.

"How can something so natural disgust you?" Price asked.

"Eating a carcass raw is not normal," I snapped weakly. All my energy had drained away from being in shock and getting sick. "That's revolting."

"Yes, well, we find humans equally disgusting."

"Really?" I narrowed my eyes at him. "Thanks, you asshole."

"Now, Trinity, don't be like that," he growled.

He grabbed my shoulders painfully. I was still standing, tied to the tree, but my feet had fallen asleep, and the sharp tingle helped keep me focused.

"This is your opportunity to be a part of history," he said.

That really got my attention. I shook my head. "What the hell are you talking about?"

He grinned, and his canines grew to their wolfish size. "The Hunt, my dear, sweet Trinity. You get to be part of the Hunt."

"The Hunt? What the fuck is that?" I asked sharply, even though I had a feeling I already knew.

"It is a most sacred tradition that many wolf packs feel is outdated." He shrugged. "But not me. I have kept the tradition going for years, and I will continue to do so with you. After all, it is the natural order of things. It's the reason we still exist at the top of the food chain." He gripped my chin hard between his thumb and index finger. "On the full moon, your heart will be a delicious prize to the strongest hunter-warrior among my pack."

Fuck. My. Life.

I glanced upward toward the stars, but clouds covered them over. A light snow was falling. It was getting colder by the hour, but I hadn't noticed with being so close to the roaring fire.

I didn't want to be here.

I wasn't ready to face this horrible reality.

When I glanced back down, Josh was still there in front of me, and the wolves were crunching away on the bones of the elk, sucking out the marrow. It was loud enough to make me sick again.

Fucking animals are going to make me go vegan again.

When I was sure I would not puke once more, I fumed, "What do I have to do with any of this?"

Josh reached out and held my face. "Good to see you still have that fight in you. You're going to need it come tomorrow night at the full moon."

Damn. This is a shituation.

He leered, pressing his naked body against mine. I grimaced and tried to pull away, but I had nowhere to go. I could tell he enjoyed it, that he wanted to keep pressing himself against me. A growl started deep in his chest and reverberated through my body. His manhood was hard against my thigh, and all the good feelings I'd had about him earlier seemed like nothing more than a prelude to this hellish nightmare.

He licked my cheek. "I know you feel the heat between us. There could be so much more, but sadly, you're not a shifter, and I don't mate with fucking humans."

I gagged at the word *mate*.

"Get the fuck off me, you bastard. Let me go. I won't tell anyone what I saw. I swear it. Just let me get out of here."

"Oh, you will get out of here, my pet," he cooed. "Don't you worry."

Josh snapped his fingers, and the rest of the wolves quickly shifted back into their human forms. They were covered in blood from head to toe, and their eyes glowed amber in the firelight. They took a step forward, and I flinched without meaning to. Josh noticed and smirked.

"It's time to explain the rules before we leave you to make peace with your destiny," he drawled.

My stomach plummeted. "Rules for what?"

"The Hunt you are about to be part of. Hunting animals is only so much fun for us. But hunting humans... Well..." He smiled. "That's been a decadent luxury for our kind for centuries. A sort of ritual," he revealed, running his fingers down my cheek.

I jerked my head away.

He grabbed my chin again, forcing me to look at him. "Tomorrow morning, I'll cut you loose, giving you a head start before I set my pack on you. If you can make it to the park rangers, you'll win, but if not, one of us will catch you, and... well..." He turned his gaze to the half-eaten elk carcass, then back.

I gulped. There was something dark in his eyes, but I was too frightened to understand what it was.

"You're going to hunt me?" I croaked. "Like a fucking animal?"

Josh laughed coldly. "What can I say? Tradition is tradition," he replied, as if we were discussing going to a baseball game. "But for now, get some sleep, my beautiful prey. For tomorrow will be the full moon, and you must run for your precious life."

My legs felt like jelly. "I don't understand. Why?" I whispered in shock. "I've done nothing to you."

"To me personally? No. But there are others—" He stopped himself and grimaced. "But you will learn all about that later. For now, just know your death will give one of my pack members the greatest honor."

This crazy motherfucker actually believed this Hunt was some great tournament of champions, and I was the human trophy.

"Rest now, Trinity. Sleep peacefully."

No. No. No.

I tried every way to rationalize what was happening, but it didn't work. No matter how much I wished myself to be somewhere else, I was tied to this fucking tree. And Josh was a shifter. And this was his pack.

I watched as they all turned back into wolves before they ripped apart what they'd left of the elk carcass.

I shuddered. Those teeth... They'd use them to tear me apart.

I was going to be sick again, but I forced myself to breathe deeply and focus on staying alive.

The rope tethered my arms to my sides, looping around my body and the tree. I kept squirming, trying to get loose, while I attempted to figure out a plan.

I tried not to smile with delight when they all disappeared from the campsite. Their blood-curdling howling echoed around the woods, but it grew farther and farther away.

Finally. Maybe I can get the hell out of here.

I wiggled from side to side, trying to loosen the rope. I was happy that I was wearing a jacket to prevent rope burn, so I continued working to loosen the rope. It was slow going, but eventually the rope slackened at the bottom just enough to where I could move my hand into the front pocket of my pants.

I sighed with relief when I felt the cold metal object. *My pocketknife.*

"Thank God. A bit of luck for me," I whispered.

Keeping my eyes pinned to the woods where they'd disappeared, I slowly used my fingertips to inch my knife up and out of my cargo pants' front pocket. My heart raced with happiness once I had it in the palm of my hand. Opening the knife, I started sawing at the rope that was around my waist.

Idiots. Did they really think I was so pathetic that I wouldn't try to escape?

As it was, I had to cut the ropes inch by painful inch. I kept my breathing steady, as I did on all my adventures, and I told myself that was exactly what this was—just another adventure.

I'd make it through this shit.

I could survive in the woods and figure out a way to get to the closest state park ranger station.

The contract with Josh was for a month. We were already a good chunk of the way into the trip, and if I didn't check in soon, someone would send help.

Yeah, Halle will make sure I'm okay.

I almost let out a cry of triumph when I finally cut through the rope at my waist. The severed rope loosened and dropped to the ground. Quietly, I walked backward into the tree line.

None of the wolves appeared in the campsite, and no eyes glowed in the darkness nearby. They were too busy howling at the moon and probably hunting more elk. After a few more steps and then a few more, I turned and sprinted deeper into the forest. I didn't pay attention to where I ran. I just took off blindly into the darkness.

This is insane.

I needed to find help, any help.

I ran and ran. My chest burned from breathing in the cold air, but I forced myself to keep going. We weren't too far from the river. If I could make it there tonight, then at least I'd have fresh water.

Would they lose my scent if I crossed it?

Part of me doubted it, but it was worth a try.

I slid to a stop in the mud and froze.

"You've got to be shitting me," I groaned in horror as a hulking form came out of the shadows.

I gulped and took a few hesitant steps back, but it was too late. The monstrous beast had seen me and was headed my way with a quick, lumbering gait. With my heart hammering and my blood thundering away in my ears, I was surprised to find I was still on my feet.

The bear turned completely around, staring into the forest. It stood on its hind legs and roared in fury. I had a second to notice the strange markings on the bear's back before it circled to face me, locking eyes on me.

It was the bear from my dreams.

When it trudged closer to me, I scrambled

back too quickly, falling onto my ass. The gigantic bear snarled in my face.

Oh damn. He's going to eat me.

I nearly pissed on myself when it sniffed my neck. Then it barked once, a small, huffed sound.

"Please," I pleaded.

Then I stopped dead when its coarse tongue licked my neck.

Holy shit.

My limbs shook, and darkness consumed me.

CHAPTER 20

FERGUS

GENTLY, I nudged her with my paw and then my nose, but she didn't move. Instinctively, I inhaled deeply to investigate her scent, just as I would with anyone I'd met for the first time.

Fuck.

The tantalizing combination of vanilla and cinnamon raced up my nostrils and shot straight to my bulging erection, making it jerk.

My bear growled, signaling that he wanted to investigate her mouthwatering scent further.

Damn. She's trouble.

I backed up to beat a hasty retreat, and then I stopped dead in my tracks. She was going to freeze to death if I left her in the mud. With one last glance around to ensure I was alone, I shifted back into a man and scooped the woman up into my arms.

The second I glanced down at her face, my heart skipped a beat. Not only was I drawn to her beauty, but I was also strangely driven to protect her.

Absolutely beautiful.

Mine, my bear growled.

Fuck no, I hissed back.

The long, dark curls that escaped her bun compelled me to run my fingers through them. Her skin was the color of mahogany, with pouty lips that begged to be plundered. Her perfect hourglass figure made my loins swell.

Damn, she's the full package.

Snowflakes fell onto her cheeks and long black eyelashes, but that didn't wake her. I could stare at her all night, and I probably would have if I hadn't remembered where we were. Just holding her in my arms sent my gut twisting and heart pounding. My beast growled in satisfaction, but I growled back with irritation. We had no time for a battle of wills.

I knew of a nearby small cave where she would at least be out of the elements and away from Price and his men until she awoke. I'd get her there and then be on my way. That was all I would do for her.

Despite what my beast thought, she was not my mate to protect. She was human and therefore under the protection of the Protectors.

But minutes later, as I was about to leave her in the small cave, I felt the strong primal urge to stay and keep her warm. And then she groaned and rolled over.

No. I have to go.

Quickly, I left the cave and shifted back into my bear.

CHAPTER 21

TRINITY

I HAD enough energy to lift my head for a moment, and I saw the shadow of a bear lumbering away.

I didn't register where I was or why a bear was there.

I was dreaming.

It was all just a dream.

Darkness overtook me, and I gratefully sank back into it, but then the howling of wolves echoed through the night, and I shot straight up.

My heart thundered away in fear.

Have they found me already?

I wrapped my arms around my legs, tucked my head down so I couldn't see or hear, and prayed to God I'd still be alive come morning.

* * *

IF YOU LOVED **GRUMPY SPECIAL OPS BEAR: EPISODE 1**, get ready for more of Fergus and Trinity's story, grab GRUMPY SPECIAL OPS BEAR: EPISODE 2 right now.

Want to binge read all of ***The Complete Grumpy Special Ops Bear Trilogy (books 1-3)***?

Grab the Complete Grumpy Special Ops Bear Trilogy!

Sign up for my Newsletter to get all my romance releases, sales, sneak peeks and a **FREE** Romance.

SNEAK PEEK AT GRUMPY SPECIAL OPS BEAR: EPISODE 2

TRINITY / CHAPTER 1

I heard something earsplitting.

I thought I was dreaming, but then I jumped as the noise grew too loud for me to ignore. It was my teeth chattering.

The cave had given me some shelter throughout the night, but I was still cold. I was fortunate I had my coat and boots, but I didn't have gloves or thermals. The cave would not keep me warm if the temperature kept dropping. Judging by the weather I'd seen before, that was likely to happen. I had no other choice. I had to make a plan, any plan, and get out of the cave.

I needed to move.

Hours had passed since I'd heard any

howling, but that meant nothing. The Hunt had begun, and I was not prepared.

The sun was barely up. The light outside the cave was pale and thin from heavy cloud cover, but at least it had stopped snowing. My limbs ached from my run through the woods, but I forced myself to stretch them out. I had to figure out which direction was south and then move as fast as I could without wearing myself out too quickly.

This was truly going to be a test of my survival skills.

After stretching, I groaned when my muscles protested. Crawling out of the cave, I was careful to check my surroundings. I spotted no footsteps in the mud, human or wolf.

But are those bear tracks?

"Maybe it wasn't just another dream." I reached out and measured my hand against the print.

Before I'd passed out, come to, and then crawled into the cave, I'd seen a bear, but I'd thought it was a figment of my imagination. It was the logical explanation anyway. But those bear tracks were huge, bigger than any I'd ever seen.

I pulled back my hand and stood. There

would be time to think about that later. I needed to move and get somewhere safe. I checked the surrounding trees, looking for moss. The moment I found some, I turned the other direction until I was facing south, the route that would take me to the state park rangers.

My pace was steady, plowing through the snow-clad trees. The last thing I wanted to do was sprain anything. I kept my gaze down to avoid any sticks or rocks, and I watched out for dips. The snow cover was only a few inches, but from the look of the clouds over-head, more would come by nightfall. My breath created little white puffs as I went. The air burned my lungs, so I forced myself to slow down.

It was definitely colder than it had been the past few days. I rubbed my arms and kept them close to my middle, but it did little to keep away the chill. There was a tear in the knee of my pants, and a draft blew right up my leg.

"Damn." I stopped to see if there was a way I could fix it.

But the tear was pretty large. I had no equipment with me to repair my pants—at least nothing that would help. Hell, I didn't even have my gloves. I'd be lucky if I didn't wind up with frostbite.

At some point, I'd have to find shelter and fresh water along with something to eat. But water had to come first. I could last a few days without food if need be. Warmth was another necessity, but I'd have to be careful with the fire. I wasn't sure how Josh Price and his pack would track me during the day.

Do they only turn at night?

How does being a wolf-shifter even work in the real world?

"Guess I should have paid more attention to those damn horror movies," I whispered. "Maybe I would have learned something useful." The thought kept me amused.

The more I kept my thoughts positive, the better off I'd be. I knew the genuine horror of my situation hadn't really sunk in yet. I was being hunted. In the light of day, it seemed like a bad dream. There was no howling or dead elk bodies torn to shreds surrounding me.

All that blood... There'd been so much of it.

I halted and turned to the side to vomit,

but all I did was dry heave. Everything else had come up last night.

I leaned against a tree as I wiped my mouth on my sleeve and took a few deep breaths to calm my stomach. I felt shaky, but I didn't have time to just stand there and hope they wouldn't find me.

It was up to me to get out of this mess. I needed to head south, find the park rangers.

I will make it.

I will survive.

***

Get ready for more of Fergus and Trinity's story, grab GRUMPY SPECIAL OPS BEAR: EPISODE 2 right now.

WANT FREE SEDONA VENEZ BOOKS?

Sign up for Sedona Venez's Newsletter and receive FREE BOOKS. In addition to the free stories, you will also get special pricing, exclusive previews and news of new releases.

GET A FREE SEDONA VENEZ BOOK!

Join Sedona's mailing list to be the first to know of new releases, free books, special prices and other author giveaways.

https://sedonavenez.com/free-book

ABOUT THE AUTHOR

USA TODAY BESTSELLING AUTHOR SEDONA VENEZ lives in New York City with her former military hubby—hooah—and their fur babies. She loves writing sizzling, sexy intricate stories about strong but broken characters who push limits, overcome their fears and risk it all for love.

Sedona loves to connect with readers!
www.sedonavenez.com